Safari Adventure
LEGOLAND®

by Carol Matas
Illustrated by Elroy Freem

A
LITTLE APPLE
PAPERBACK

SCHOLASTIC INC.
New York Toronto London Auckland Sydney

For Preben Dewald, with thanks

The author would like to thank Perry Nodelman
for his helpful critique,
Eva Moore for her insightful editing,
and Donna Badcock
for the typing of the manuscript.

ISBN 0-590-45876-0

12 11 10 9 8 7 6 5 4 3 2   3 4 5 6 7 8/9

Printed in the U.S.A.   28

First Scholastic printing, March 1993

Contents

1

THE
SAFARI PARK

"I get to steer!" Aaron yelled as he and Rebecca climbed into the Safari Park jeep. The jeep was black-and-white-striped like a zebra. It looked just like a Lego car except instead of being two inches tall, this one was big enough for two people to ride in.

Aaron could tell that Rebecca wanted to steer, but she felt twelve years old was too old to fight over such a thing. She sat down beside him, a big frown on her face. Aaron was eight, just the right age for a ride like this. The man in charge of the ride took their tickets, then started their car, which ran on tracks leading them through the Safari Park.

Aaron, Rebecca, and their mom and dad were all on a visit to Legoland in Denmark. Aaron's grandparents lived in Denmark, and the whole family had come over this summer to visit them.

As a special part of their trip they had come to Legoland. But the trip had become *very* special for Aaron because on their first night he had had a most amazing adventure. He had heard someone calling for help and had gone out alone to find the voice. That's how he'd discovered that Legoland came alive at night. Titania's Palace, a fairy palace, was the home of *real* fairies, and he had rescued the fairy prince, Aryeh, from Bad Bart of Legoredo.

As the ride started and Aaron looked eagerly around him, he wondered whether it had all been an incredible dream. But then he felt the little jacket that Queen Titania had given him, which was now in his pocket, and he knew it was all real! Aaron had actually been small enough to wear the jacket because he'd been magically shrunk to the size of Lego people during his night adventure. He'd come back to his real size in the morning. He looked at the animals in the Safari Park and wondered whether they, too, came alive at night. *That* would be exciting because these animals were big — almost life size — even though they were completely made out of Lego blocks.

There were giraffes and zebras, elephants and ostriches, monkeys, snakes, rhinoceroses — even vultures. Some animals stood under trees. Some, like the monkeys, sat on rocks. Flamingos waded in a little lake.

Aaron let go of the wheel and reached into his pocket. (He didn't *really* have to steer because the jeep ran on train tracks; he was only pretending.) He pulled his Lego gun out of his pocket. His mom didn't allow him to own a toy gun, so he'd made himself one out of Legos. He often carried it with him so he could play with it.

Aaron pointed the Lego gun at the elephant. "Bang, bang," he shouted.

"Oh stop it!" Rebecca grumbled. "It's not funny to shoot animals."

Aaron ignored her. She always said that. But he dreamed of being a big game hunter with a real gun and going into the jungle to shoot wild animals.

"Bang!" he screamed, aiming and shooting at the lions. "Bang! Got it!"

Rebecca rolled her eyes. Aaron aimed his toy gun and fired at all the animals until the ride was over. Their parents were waiting for them as they scrambled out of the car.

"I'm not going on any more rides with you if you keep doing that," Rebecca declared. "It's sickening."

"I'm just pretending!" Aaron objected.

Rebecca snorted and turned her back.

"What's the matter?" their mom asked.

"Nothing," both kids replied. They always fought with each other, but they tried not to tattle to their parents. Aaron put the Lego gun back in his pocket so his mom and dad wouldn't see it.

"Well then," his dad said, "what's next?"

They all paused for a minute as they tried to decide where to go. There was so much to choose from!

Legoland is a big amusement park where everything is made from Lego blocks or looks like Legos. There is a western town, Legoredo, Duploland, which is full of rides, and, of course, Miniland. Miniland is made up of exhibits like an airport with runways, planes, and airport buildings, or parts of a city like Copenhagen or a Norwegian fiord or Dutch windmills. Miniland is built just the right size for Lego people, but no one knows that the Lego people come alive at night and actually live there — no one but Aaron, that is.

After everyone stopped to think, they all started to talk at once.

"Let's go on the rollercoaster at Legoredo," Aaron exclaimed.

"Let's go to the pirate exhibit," Rebecca suggested.

"How about Titania's Palace?" said their mom.

"I'm hungry," their dad said. "I vote for a restaurant."

Their mom laughed.

"Okay," she said. "First the pirate exhibit, then the rollercoaster, then the restaurant, and then Titania's Palace. I'm glad we decided to stay another day. There's so much to do."

Everyone agreed. Aaron especially wanted to see Titania's Palace again. He knew his friend Prince Aryeh would be sleeping now, but tonight, when Aaron went to bed, Aryeh would wake up.

I wonder what Aryeh is doing to-night? Aaron thought. Maybe I'll go and see.

2
THE
GOLDEN SAILBOAT

Night had fallen. Aaron and his family were fast asleep, but there was activity in Titania's Palace.

Titania's Palace was one of the indoor exhibits at Legoland. It stood in the middle of a large room and looked like an elaborate dollhouse on a pedestal. Everything was in miniature and very beautiful.

Prince Aryeh was very much awake. At eight years old, he looked remarkably like Aaron, with fair hair and blue eyes (except, of course, Aryeh had translucent fairy wings attached at *his* back). He was standing in the entrance hall of the palace, between the grand mahogany staircases, under the glass chandelier, having a serious talk with his mother.

"Please, Mother," Aryeh pleaded, "I know I'm big enough."

"Aryeh," Queen Titania said, "it's true you are very big. But this is no ordinary trophy. It was made by your great-great-grandfather, Oberon." Queen Titania held up a beautiful gold replica of a sailboat. "This will be the first-place prize for the sailing regatta. Although the trophy is kept at the palace, the winner's name will be engraved on it. What would we do if it got lost? I am flying over to the race site in a few hours. I shall take it with me."

"But, Mother, let *me* do it. It's so boring waiting around here for everyone to get ready. And you know you'll have lots of other things to carry. I *heard* you tell Martha that you had too many things to take, and you asked her to take the trophy, but she's busy baking so why won't you let me?" Aryeh stopped for a minute to catch his breath. "You just don't trust me! You think I can't do it."

Queen Titania smiled. "Well, Aryeh, I do have lots of other things to take. And of course I trust you. Here it is." And she handed him the gold sailboat.

"Thank you!" Aryeh said. "And don't worry. I'll fly straight over there. You won't be sorry!"

Before the Queen had a chance to change her mind, Prince Aryeh flew out of the palace, through the room, and outside into Legoland.

Legoland was all lit up so brightly it might have been the middle of the day. Aryeh had to carry the trophy over to the waterways around the Statue of

Liberty, a large replica of the real statue made entirely out of Legos. That was where the race was to be held.

Aryeh was having a good time. He flew over Miniland, the German castles, the city of Copenhagen, the airport, the Copenhagen harbor, the Dutch windmills, and finally, the edge of the Safari Park. He could see the Statue of Liberty getting closer and closer. Beneath him, planes took off and landed (one flew right past him), and ships moved. Lego people were busy at their nightly tasks.

Boy, Aryeh thought, I've flown this way hundreds of times with Mother or Father or one of my older sisters. I could practically do it with my eyes closed. Why does Mother always worry? And just for fun, he did close his eyes. Just for a second. He opened them when he heard a blood-chilling screech.

Diving in, almost upon him, was a vulture from the Safari Park. It was huge, with a bald head, a black body with a white ruffle of feathers around the neck, gray claws, and a sharp gray beak.

Aryeh was so surprised and so terrified when this great bird flew at him that he threw up his hands to protect his face — and dropped the trophy! Down, down it went into the Safari Park. But Aryeh couldn't go after it — he had to get away from the vulture, which screeched and shrieked and swooped at him again.

Aryeh pumped his wings and darted this way and that until he was beyond the Safari Park. He hovered over the calm scene of the Dutch windmills rotating in the breeze. The animals from the Safari Park never left the Safari grounds, so he knew he was safe. He floated to the ground and sank onto the warm grass. He was panting so hard, he could hardly breathe. But he could think, and all he could think of was the trophy!

How could he tell his mother he'd lost the golden sailboat? She'd never let him do anything grown-up again. He'd be treated like a baby the rest of his life. He put his head in his hands and groaned. What a mess! What a terrible mess!

Well, he had to go back and get it. But he couldn't help thinking of that vulture. If only there were someone who could go searching with him. Just so he didn't have to go alone ... And then he thought of his friend Aaron!

Aaron had saved him from Bad Bart yesterday. Maybe he could help him again. But hadn't Aaron said he was going home today? Well, there was only one way to find out. He'd go to the hotel and see if his friend was still there. Quickly, Aryeh darted into the air and flew back the way he'd come.

3
LEGOLAND
AT NIGHT

"Aaron, Aaron, wake up!"

Aaron sat up with a jolt.

"Who's there?" he exclaimed.

The voice was tiny and thin.

"It's me, Aryeh! Over here."

Aaron turned his head and sure enough, there was his friend Aryeh, flying around just about at eye level, his wings beating the air. Aaron always made his mother leave the bathroom light on with the door open a crack so it wasn't pitch dark in the room. He couldn't see Aryeh well, but he could make him out though the Prince was only around two inches tall.

16

"What are you doing here?" Aaron asked, feeling very surprised.

"It wasn't easy finding your room," Aryeh replied, "I can tell you that. I had to wait until the person at the front desk went away, and then I had to find your name in the computer. My fingers are too small to make the keys work so I had to jump on them one by one."

He flew closer and Aaron could see that he was panting from flying so fast and that he looked really upset.

"Can you come with me?"

"Now?"

"Now would be excellent."

"Why?"

"I need your help." Aryeh looked at Aaron's sleeping family. "Perhaps we should talk on our way. We don't have much time."

Aaron's sister Rebecca stirred in her bed.

"We'd better hurry," Aryeh said. "Your parents won't wake up because they can't. They don't believe in magic so they can't see me. But your sister just might, and then we'll have so much explaining to do that we'll never get out of here! And I'm in an awful rush."

"Okay," Aaron agreed, and he quickly changed into the same pants he'd had on during the day and his Blue Jays sweatshirt. He put on his sneakers and then tiptoed to the door. Then he remembered something. He picked up the room key from the table by the door and slipped it into his pocket. Now he could get back into the room without waking anyone. Quietly he opened the door and let Aryeh fly out, then he stepped out and closed the door softly behind him. It was just after one in the morning and the hallways were empty.

"If I could sit on you until we get to the palace, it would be much quicker," Aryeh suggested. "I would have to fly *very* fast to try to keep up with you."

"Sure," Aaron agreed as Aryeh settled down on his shoulder. "Hold on," Aaron said.

"Don't worry," Aryeh laughed. "I can't fall!"

Aaron hurried down the empty hallway, past the restaurant and the hotel foyer, and up the stairs which led to the passageway connecting the hotel and Legoland. The passageway was full of Lego figures behind glass — Lego soldiers, Lego pandas, Lego Vikings, Lego penguins, Lego cats and dogs.

During the day, the figures stood still

and unmoving. Now they were all alive. They were talking or barking or practicing sword fights. The whole passageway was so noisy, Aaron was tempted to plug his ears. But when they saw him, they suddenly stopped. Everything went quiet. Aaron hurried past them feeling very self-conscious.

"They aren't used to seeing big people at night," Aryeh told him. "You know, big people aren't allowed in Legoland at night because they could easily squash someone. You're probably the first one they've ever seen."

"But they see lots of us during the day," Aaron said.

"Their eyes may be open," Aryeh said, "but they are really asleep most of the time."

As soon as they started down the stairs on the far side, the hubbub started again, but this time it was even louder.

"That will give them something to talk about for years," Aryeh chuckled.

By now, Aaron knew the way well. He hurried through the indoor exhibits, a room showing how Lego blocks are made, and a room full of old-fashioned toys, some of which were mechanical. They moved and whirred and clanged.

Titania's Palace was in the next room. It seemed empty, just like it did during the day.

"Where is everyone?" Aaron asked.

"Well, that's what I have to tell you," Aryeh replied. "We have to go to the Safari Park. Wait here. I'll go get the shrinking potion." And he flew into the palace.

Aaron stood by himself and waited for his friend. Well, here he was for the second night in a row about to embark on another adventure. But why did his friend need his help? What was going on? And why did they have to go to the Safari Park?

4
AARON SHRINKS

Aaron waited impatiently for his friend to return.

Soon Aryeh was flying in front of him, holding a small cup in his hand.

"Here's the shrinking potion," he said to Aaron. "Please hurry!"

Well, Aaron thought, if Aryeh thinks it's so urgent, it must be. He took the little cup and put it to his lips. A couple of drops of sweet liquid slid down his throat, and then he felt like the room was getting very big. In one big swoosh he was a tiny person standing very close to the cold floor, just as he had been the night before.

Aryeh flew back to the castle and returned with a bicycle in his arms.

"Whew!" he said, putting it down beside Aaron. "That was heavy. Well," he continued, looking at Aaron, "get on!"

"Why?" Aaron asked.

"Because we're in a terrible hurry, and you can't walk as fast as I can fly. So I had the idea that you could ride my bike."

"But *why?*" Aaron repeated.

"Well," explained Aryeh, "I'm in a lot of trouble. And I need your help to get out of it."

"What is it?!" Aaron exclaimed, getting a little angry at Aryeh for taking so long to tell him.

"Come on," Aryeh answered. "I'll tell you as we go. That way we won't waste time. We have almost *no* time at all now. The sailboat race starts in two hours!"

Aaron sighed. He figured he had better do as the Prince suggested or he would *never* hear what the trouble was! He picked up the bike, which was a beautiful two-wheeler and just the right size for him. He got on.

"Okay. I'm ready. You lead. I'll follow."

"We'll go through those doors," the Prince pointed, "into the park. Then we'll travel through a small part of Miniland to the Safari Park. And when we've finished what we have to do there, I must be at the Statue of Liberty by 3:30 A.M."

Aaron began to peddle. The Prince flew beside him and talked as they went.

"The Statue of Liberty?" Aaron said. "Rebecca and I had a ride in the little boats there yesterday." That is what Aaron said out loud. Inside he was really thinking about the Safari Park.

"Well," Aryeh continued, "the race is very important. And I just *know* I can win. But I can't show my face because of what's happened."

"What?" Aaron asked again. "What's happened?"

Quickly Aryeh told Aaron all about the trophy and how he had lost it. When he finished, Aaron understood why Aryeh was so worried.

"But," Aaron answered, "if you explain to your mom what happened, she won't be mad. It's not your fault about the vulture."

"That's just it!" Aryeh exclaimed. "She won't be mad, but she'll think she was right in the first place and that I'm too young to be trusted! Don't you see? I just have to get it back. And without anyone knowing that anything went wrong. That's why I asked you to come." He dropped his voice to a whisper. "I didn't want to go into the Safari Park alone."

Aaron certainly understood now why his friend needed his help. His own parents, his teachers, and all the adults he knew always thought he was too young for anything! They never trusted him! He knew just how Aryeh felt and why he didn't want his mom to find out. Of course he had to help him.

Aaron felt in the pocket of his pants. He pulled out his Lego gun. He was thrilled.

"A safari!" he exclaimed. "If any wild animals come at me, I'll shoot them down! This is great! I've always wanted to do this!"

Aryeh looked at the gun.

"Aaron, you have to be careful with that. It's nighttime and you're in Legoland. That will work like a *real* gun

here, with bullets and everything."

"All the better!" Aaron said. "Just let that vulture come after us!" He pointed the gun in the air. "Bang! Bang! You're dead!"

"Put it away for now, Aaron," Aryeh begged. "I'm sure we won't need it. I'll fly in the air, you look on the ground, and with any luck, we'll find the trophy before the vulture finds us."

Aaron put the gun away. A little part of him felt very nervous about going into the Safari Park. The animals would be huge! After all, even at his regular size, the animals were much larger than he. But at only two inches tall, they'd be more like mountains than animals — moving mountains. But hadn't he always wanted to go on a safari adventure? He told himself not to be silly, and followed Aryeh out into the Legoland Park.

5
THE CREATURE

"Why did you fly so close to the Safari Park?" Aaron asked Prince Aryeh. He was curious about how the accident had happened. "Couldn't you have gone a safer way?"

Prince Aryeh look wounded by the suggestion.

"That," he replied, "is something my mother would say."

Aaron almost blushed. He realized that it did sound a bit like that.

"It's no fun to fly over the restaurant," Aryeh continued. "I love to fly over the Safari Park and look at the animals. I especially like to watch the monkeys play. They're so funny!"

Aaron agreed with the Prince. It was fun to watch monkeys.

"And, you see, the vultures usually fly around the part of the park that's near Legoredo. That's where their nest is. Don't know what they were doing on this side of the park," he grumbled. "It wasn't fair!"

Aaron sighed. "I know just what you mean," he agreed. "Whenever I try to do something that's fun, I always seem to end up in trouble. It *isn't* fair."

Aryeh smiled at his friend. It certainly was nice to be with someone who understood.

The two boys traveled down the large road which led into Miniland. Aaron was glad to be in the part of Legoland that was built for people of his present size. He no longer felt too small. It was wonderful to see all the buildings he'd seen when he was big, up so close. They were very beautiful.

The boys passed castles and the airport, and the harbor of Nyhavn. The Dutch windmills moved in the breeze.

Aaron thought that one day it would be nice to come and visit Aryeh and just go into all the castles and have a real tour, like a sightseer. Also, he desperately wanted to stop for a hot dog at the hot dog stand, but he knew they had to hurry. And he would have loved to go into the Queen of Legoland's castle. She *had* promised him he could. But, again, he knew now was no time to think about that. He had to think about helping Aryeh find the trophy.

"How big is this gold sailboat?" he asked the Prince.

"Not big," replied Aryeh. "I can easily carry it if I use both hands."

Aaron sighed. That was bad. It

wouldn't be easy to spot it, then.

"What's our plan?" he said. "We should have a plan."

"Well," the Prince suggested, "I thought that once we got to the Safari Park you could see if you are able to spot the trophy from the ground, and I'll fly around and see if I can spot it from the air!"

"Couldn't we ask the animals?" Aaron suggested.

"Unfortunately, they don't speak. They're really just like animals anywhere. And because of the way they're made — so realistically — when they come to life, they move naturally — not like the Lego people."

Aaron knew what Aryeh meant. Most of the Lego people walked stiffly because they couldn't bend their knees or elbows.

Aaron was enjoying the bike ride.

People looked at him curiously as he and Aryeh traveled down the road because he obviously wasn't a Lego creature and he had no wings, so he wasn't a fairy either. Some were so curious that their heads turned all the way around on their bodies as they watched Aaron pedal past.

A dog barked and jumped in circles. Since it couldn't twist its Lego body, each turn took two jumps: It sprang into the air, landed halfway around, jumped again, and landed all the way around. It did this over and over again. Aaron thought maybe his owner should try training it to be calmer, but then he remembered Jake, his own dog who had had to stay home in Canada.

He missed Jake terribly. Jake, he remembered, was just as noisy as this dog. He barked at everybody and everything, and no one could make him stop.

He would certainly bark at this dog if he could ever see him.

Finally the boys arrived at the outskirts of the Safari Park. In front of them was the ride he and Rebecca had been on that afternoon, the little black-and-white-striped jeeps which ran on train tracks. The tracks had seemed very small to Aaron when he was big, but now, as he and Aryeh got closer, he realized that he could never get the bicycle over them.

"I could lift it over," said Aryeh, "but you won't really be able to ride in the park. It's too grassy."

Aaron realized that Aryeh was right. The grass was cut short, but it still came quite high up on their legs since they were so small. It would be too hard to ride the bike.

"What should we do with it?" Aaron asked. "You don't want to get into more trouble with your mom for losing your bike."

"Oh," Aryeh said, not the least bit worried, "we can just leave it here. I'll come back and get it tomorrow. As long as we hide it carefully under a tree so a big person doesn't see it or step on it or something, it'll be fine."

"Aren't you worried someone will steal it?" Aaron asked. His bike at home had to be locked up every second.

"Here? Oh, no," Aryeh laughed. "The only people here who steal things are the pirates, and they wouldn't be interested in a bike. They only like gold and jewels and that sort of thing."

Aaron looked around. There was a group of small bushes near the tracks.

"Over there?" he asked.

"Perfect," Aryeh agreed.

The boys hid the bike. Then Aaron walked up to the train track. It was as high as his waist, and slippery. He could never have gotten over the track without Aryeh's help. Aryeh beat his wings very hard and pulled Aaron up into the air until Aaron cleared the track. Then Aryeh let go, and Aaron crashed down onto the other side. Aaron walked over the wooden slats and Aryeh helped him over the other track. Finally they stood looking out at the Safari Park.

And then Aaron heard noises. The roar of a lion. The trumpet of an elephant. The hiss of a snake. The gurgle of a . . . what was that noise?

Slowly Aaron and Aryeh turned to their left. And there, staring at them with beady eyes, was the strangest creature Aaron had ever seen. It was made entirely from Lego blocks. It had a square head made out of yellow Legos with long antennae attached to the top

of its head. It had about ten legs, all made from different-colored Legos, and a long, rectangular blue, red, and yellow body. It had a black tail that stuck straight up in the air. The creature growled.

"What's that?" Aaron whispered.

"Sometimes, a kid will make something out of the Legos put out in bins all over the park for children to play with," Aryeh whispered back, "then set it down and forget about it. But this time I think the kid who made this creature was very proud of it, and felt it belonged here in the Safari Park."

How would the kid know, Aaron thought, that his or her creation would come alive at night. Still, I wish whoever it was had made a nice tree instead!

And then the creature began to move slowly toward the two boys!

6

SAFARI BILL

"Okay," whispered Aaron, "I have a plan."

"What?" hissed Aryeh.

"You fly, and I RUN!!"

And with that, the two boys took off. Aaron ran as fast as he could, with Aryeh flying just overhead.

"You're losing him, you're losing him!" Aryeh cried. "Just keep . . . oh!"

"Oh!" Aaron echoed.

To Aaron it seemed that he was suddenly looking at a tree, but it was smooth and yellow with a little gray at the bottom. Actually there were four trees just like that. He looked up and then bent backwards to look higher.

"Giraffe!" Aryeh shouted down at him.

"Well," Aaron muttered, "that's better than the other creature."

But just as he finished speaking, the ground around him seemed to shake. The giraffe was walking.

"Unless you get stepped on," Aaron screamed, "then it's not better."

And so he had to run again. But this time he had to turn and twist and dodge. And then, right after the large giraffe walked past him, a slightly smaller one followed, and Aaron had to dodge that one as well.

Once the giraffes were safely past, Aaron sank down onto the grass. After all, it was the middle of the night for him, he had just had quite a long bike ride and then quite a fast, hard run. He was tired!

Aryeh settled down onto the grass beside him.

"Ouch!" Aryeh exclaimed.

"What's the matter?" Aaron asked, worried.

"I don't know," Aryeh answered. "It's my wing. Something feels funny. When the giraffe surprised us like that, I almost ran into it, and I twisted around very fast and crashed into a tree!" At that point he twisted to show Aaron what he'd done. . . . "Ouch! And now it hurts."

"Let me see," said Aaron.

Aryeh tried to spread his wings to fly, but the wing drooped and wouldn't move. It seemed to be broken.

"Ouch!" Aryeh exclaimed again. "This is bad! I won't be able to fly with just one wing."

"Maybe we'd better go back to the palace and get help," Aaron said.

Aryeh grimaced. "I don't *want* to go back. I have to find that trophy." He got up and walked a few steps. "It doesn't hurt at all when I'm walking." He tried to move the wing. "Ouch! Only when I move it. Well, we'll just both have to look on the ground. But I won't give up!"

"Where should we look, then?" Aaron asked.

"It *should* be somewhere around here. In this area," Aryeh replied.

"What animals live in this area?" Aaron asked, wondering if he'd get a chance to hunt some, just like on a safari. (He was a little ashamed of the way he'd run away from that odd creature and he vowed *never* to do that again!)

"Lions," said Aryeh.

"Great!"

"Zebras."

"They're okay."

"Gnus."

"What's a gnu?"

"Well, it has horns, and a big black stripe down its nose, and a funny gray beard, and it's a bit bigger than a zebra."

"Oh yes," said Aaron, "I know the ones you mean."

"But," Aryeh said, "it's not really that simple. You see, all the animals move around freely at night. So who knows who or what we'll bump into."

"Or," Aaron whispered, "who or what will bump into *us*. What's that noise?"

Both boys held their breath. It sounded as if something was moving through the jungle. They heard twigs cracking and strange little noises. And then, bursting out from behind a tree came a Lego man, dressed from head to toe in safari gear — high brown boots, a brown jacket, and a large beige safari hat. The man was holding a rifle and had a very fierce expression on his face. He glared at them.

"Now, what are two youngsters like you doing out in these dangerous parts?" he demanded.

At first the boys were so surprised by him they didn't answer. But after a moment Aryeh stood up and said, "And who, my dear sir, are you?"

Aryeh's tone of voice reminded Aaron that his friend really was a prince.

"Me? Why," the man said, jerking his Lego arm out so quickly Aaron was afraid it might snap off, "I am Safari Bill!"

"Safari Bill?" Aryeh repeated.

"You got it, youngster! I travel these jungles with my trusty rifle and hunt these big wild animals. I'm brave. There's none braver. An elephant fifty

times my size won't scare me! I suppose you've heard all about me and would like my autograph," he added.

"Well," the Prince replied, "I'm afraid I've *never* heard of you."

"Excuse me, Safari Bill," Aaron said, "but could I see your gun?"

Safari Bill proudly displayed the rifle for Aaron. Aaron pulled his out of his pocket.

"I have a gun, too," he said. "When you go hunting, can I come along?"

"Aaron!" Aryeh exclaimed. "What about the trophy?"

"Oh," Aaron said, very disappointed. "For a minute I forgot all about it. I mean, look Aryeh, a real hunter! This is so exciting!"

"Yes," said Safari Bill, "it is exciting just to be around me. Why, that's my middle name — Excitement. Safari Excitement Bill they may as well call me.

I stalk the fiercest animals known to man. Well now, can't stay and chat. I must go and shoot something!" And off he stalked.

"Come on, Aryeh," Aaron urged. "We'll just follow him for a minute."

"We certainly will," Aryeh exclaimed. "We have to stop him! He can't shoot the animals here. They have as much right to be here as he does!"

So for different reasons the two boys ran after Safari Bill, both calling, "Wait, wait!"

7
LIONS AND ELEPHANTS

Of course, when Safari Bill said he crept through the jungle silently, that was hardly the truth. Like most Lego figures, he couldn't bend his legs at the knees, so he walked in a jerky motion. First one leg swung out and crashed down on the ground. Then the other leg did the same thing.

Safari Bill crashed into a clearing where a lion was resting beside a large rock. The lion heard him coming and turned a pair of lazy brown eyes on him. Safari Bill raised his rifle. Then he ran right up to the lion.

Aryeh called out in his best prince's voice. "I demand you leave that animal alone!"

But Safari Bill pointed his rifle at the space between the beautiful lion's eyes and fired!

Aaron and Aryeh gasped and closed their eyes. Silence. When they opened their eyes again, they couldn't believe what they saw.

A rubber suction cup attached to a string was stuck onto the lion's forehead. Safari Bill's rifle was a pop gun! Of course, since the lion was made of Legos, he had no real fur and his surface was smooth, so the suction cup stuck very well.

Safari Bill roared at the lion.

"Come quietly now, sir; admit defeat. I am Safari Bill, the greatest hunter alive. You must accept defeat."

The lion yawned. He looked at Safari Bill and then up at the little rubber cup stuck to his forehead. With one swat of his mighty paw he batted the suction cup off his forehead and sent it flying through the air. Since the string was attached to the rifle, and Safari Bill was holding tightly to the rifle, Safari Bill followed the string and flew through the air, too. He could have kept flying for a very long time if a big tree had not been in his way. He bounced off the tree and landed on his back in the high grass.

The lion got up, stretched, and looked at Aaron and Aryeh for a moment, as if they weren't very interesting. Then he walked slowly away, probably in search of a quieter place to relax.

Aaron and Aryeh ran over to Safari Bill. He grinned up at them.

"Now do you believe me?" he said

proudly, as they helped him up. "Have you ever seen such bravery in the face of such a ferocious beast?"

Aaron was disappointed. Safari Bill wasn't a real hunter after all! He could see Aryeh was trying not to laugh.

"You could have been hurt," Aryeh said sincerely. "Don't you think you should be more careful?"

"Careful?" Safari Bill laughed. "Careful is not a word in my vocabulary." He turned his head suddenly. "Quiet!" he commanded the boys.

"What is it?" Aaron asked.

"Don't you feel it?" Safari Bill replied.

Aaron did feel something. The earth was beginning to shake.

"The elephant," declared Safari Bill, as he readied his gun for another attack. "The greatest animal a hunter can face. Good-bye, young sirs. I must hunt this beast."

And off he strode, through the grass.

Aaron turned to Aryeh.

"We have to stop him. He'll get hurt."

Aryeh smiled. "It's very difficult for a Lego person to actually get hurt, but the way Safari Bill is behaving, he'll find a way. You're right, we'd better try to stop him."

"He's only as tall as the elephant's foot," Aaron said. "How on earth does he think he can hunt an elephant?"

Aryeh laughed. "I think he thinks he can do anything!"

Aaron and Aryeh hurried after Safari Bill. They saw him run into a large clearing full of grass and low bushes. The elephant must have been in a hurry to get somewhere, however, because within seconds the boys saw it

looming high in the air, coming closer
and closer. They both dived aside and
just missed being trampled by the animal's huge feet.

When the elephant had passed, trum-
peting as it went, Aryeh and Aaron
scrambled to their feet and hurried to
where they had last seen Safari Bill.
But he was nowhere to be found! So
they began to call for him.

"Safari Bill! Safari Bill! Are you all
right?"

"Maybe we should call him Mr. Safari," Aryeh suggested, when he didn't
answer. "Perhaps he thinks we're being
rude!"

"Or maybe his suction cup is stuck to
the elephant, and he's being pulled
along right now," Aaron said.

"Excuse me," said a voice.

Aaron and Aryeh jumped with sur-
prise.

"Did you hear something?" Aaron asked.

"Here, lads," the voice spoke.

Aaron and Aryeh looked around, very puzzled. There were no trees in this small clearing. They heard a voice. And, yet, where could Safari Bill be? They could not see him anywhere in the grass.

"Look down, youngsters."

The boys followed the sound. And suddenly Aaron almost tripped over Safari Bill's hat.

"Don't ruin my hat," Safari Bill cried. "Be careful."

"Why, he's straight down in the ground!" Aaron exclaimed.

"The elephant must have stomped on him," Aryeh said. "Stomped him right into the ground!"

Aryeh bent down. "Are you all right, Mr. Safari Bill?" he asked.

"Of course I am, lad," he replied. "And drop the mister. Would you mind terribly getting me out?"

"We'll have to dig him out," Aaron declared.

Aryeh nodded. The boys looked at each other. Then they looked at Safari Bill's head. And they both started to laugh. But very quietly so as not to hurt his feelings.

They quickly removed enough dirt from around Safari Bill's head and shoulders and arms so they could help pull him out. He stood before them and shook both their hands.

"Boys," he said, "you've saved me and now I will never leave your sides. It's a code of honor. Until I can save you, we're together forever."

"No, no, I assure you," the Prince said, "that really isn't necessary. And we have to go now because we're looking for something."

"Then lead on, young sirs. I will follow!"

Aaron and Aryeh sighed. They were running out of time now and knew Safari Bill would just keep getting into trouble. Still, they had no choice and couldn't say anything in front of him, so they walked along and continued their search for the trophy.

Suddenly Aaron called, "What's that?"

The boys, with Safari Bill following them, reached an area which had more trees and boulders.

"Eeeek. Aak. Eueg!" A loud shrieking noise pierced the air. Swinging through the trees and jumping up and down was a group of monkeys. Aaron counted four of them. He stood, rooted to the

spot. They were playing catch — with a very bright, shiny object.

"Aryeh," whispered Aaron, "could it be?"

Aryeh whispered back.

"It *could* and it *is*. That's the trophy! But how will we ever get it back from them?"

8

THE MONKEYS

"I'll get it back for you!" Safari Bill announced. And then he added, "What is *it* anyway?"

Quickly Aryeh explained to Safari Bill about the trophy, why they needed it back, and why they were in such a hurry. He also introduced himself and Aaron to Safari Bill and explained about his broken wing.

Safari Bill shouldered his rifle.

"I'll just hunt down all those monkeys for you," he declared. "No problem."

Aaron and Aryeh grabbed him.

"No!" Aryeh objected. "Please. Let us do it!"

"Never!" Safari Bill replied. "You need my help."

The boys were desperate. They knew that if the monkeys got scared or ran away they would lose all chance of getting the trophy to the race on time.

"His legs!" Aryeh cried to Aaron.

"What?" Aaron said.

"Grab his legs," Aryeh ordered.

Aaron trusted his friend and so he tackled Safari Bill by the legs. Since Lego figures are so stiff, Safari Bill immediately fell forward onto his face. Aryeh grabbed one of the hunter's legs and pulled. It came right off.

"Stop!" Aaron called. "You're hurting him!"

"Not a bit," Aryeh assured him. "But

removing one leg *will* keep him from getting in our way."

"The young Prince is correct," Safari Bill said, although his voice was a little muffled as his face was in the grass. "I am not hurt, but I am unable to help you now."

The Prince put Safari Bill's leg behind a tree so it wouldn't get lost. Then he and Aaron helped the Lego man sit up beside another tree.

"I'm sorry," Aryeh said to him, "but we really need to *think* about this, not just rush into anything."

"You're making a big mistake, lad," Safari Bill sighed. "But you are young and so I forgive you."

"Thank you," Aryeh replied gravely. He motioned Aaron away from Safari Bill so they could think of an idea without constantly being interrupted.

Naturally, they were both delighted

to have found the trophy. But, as Aaron said, it was definitely a good news, bad news situation. The good news was that they could see the trophy from where they sat. The bad news was they might never get it back!

"Monkeys love shiny things," Aryeh sighed. "They'll never give it up."

"There *must* be something we can do to get it away from them," Aaron said. "We just have to think. Very hard."

"If only we had the time!" Aryeh said.

"Maybe they would trade it for something," Aaron suggested. "Something else bright and shiny."

"That's a great idea!" Aryeh exclaimed. "I've got lots of things at home that are even shinier than that!"

Then the boys looked at each other and groaned.

"Except you can't fly home because of your wing," Aaron said.

"Right," sighed the Prince.

"And if you could fly," Aaron continued, "you could just wait until they were throwing it and snatch it away, right in the air."

"But I can't fly," Aryeh grumbled.

"I told you you should let me help!" Safari Bill called. The boys ignored him. They stared as the monkeys continued to play and shriek and throw the tiny golden boat back and forth.

"We have to figure out something!" Aaron exclaimed in frustration. "Okay. Monkeys like shiny things. We don't have a shiny thing to trade. What else do they like?"

"They like to play," his friend said.

"That's true," Aaron agreed. "Well," he suggested, "do you think they'd play with us? Maybe we could get them to *forget* about the trophy."

"Good idea!" Aryeh answered. "Hey . . . you know any good songs?"

"Why?" Aaron replied.

"That might be a way to get their attention. Can you dance?"

Aaron shook his head. His mother had wanted him to take dance lessons, but he had insisted on playing hockey instead.

"I can, of course," said the Prince. "What songs do you know?"

Aaron thought. He knew some rock and roll songs. But he didn't think Prince Aryeh would know them. Even though the Prince spoke perfect English, he'd probably know Danish rock and roll, not English rock and roll.

"Rap?" Aaron asked.

Aryeh shook his head. "Beatles?" he asked.

"Yes!" Aaron exclaimed. "I know all

that stuff. My mom and dad listen to it all the time. But do yours? After all, you are royalty. I would think you would only listen to Beethoven or Mozart and stuff like that."

"We listen to classical music, certainly," Aryeh agreed. "But," he grinned, "we also listen to The Beatles!"

But when they compared, the boys found they both knew different Beatles songs. Aryeh knew "Roll Over, Beethoven" and Aaron knew "Twist and Shout."

"This is stupid," Aaron said. "We must both know at least *one* song that's the same, or we'll have to sing 'Happy Birthday.'"

Aryeh laughed.

"The monkeys won't know *what* we're singing. 'Happy Birthday' will do as well as anything!"

Aaron laughed, too. Then he took a deep breath.

"Okay," he said. "Let's go. We both sing 'Happy Birthday' as loud as we can, and you dance, and I'll run around, and we'll get their attention. Then we'll see what happens!"

Aryeh nodded. The boys got up and ran out from under the small tree. They began to sing "Happy birthday to you" at the top of their lungs. Aaron's loud voice, which always got him in trouble, made the monkeys look down. All four of them stopped playing. They stared at the little dolls on the ground. And then slowly they all dropped down onto the ground until they were standing in a circle around the boys.

"Happy birthday to you!" shrieked Aaron and Aryeh. Aryeh danced. Aaron jumped around. "Happy birthday to you!"

And then the largest monkey of the group reached down slowly and picked the boys up, one in each hand.

"I think we got their attention!" Aaron screamed to Aryeh.

"I think you're right," Aryeh screamed back, as the boys were lifted higher and higher so the monkey could take a good look at them!

9
PLAYING TRICKS

Aaron stared into the big brown eyes of the monkey. At first he'd been terrified as the large hand scooped him up and lifted him higher and higher. His heart had pounded so hard that he was afraid it would explode. But when he looked into the monkey's eyes, a lot of the fear left him. The eyes were soft and nice and seemed more curious than anything else.

Aaron tried to smile. He waved at the monkey. Aryeh was in the monkey's other hand. "He seems nice," Aaron called to Aryeh.

"As long as he doesn't decide to play

catch with us," Aryeh shouted back.

The monkey seemed startled to hear their voices so close up. Slowly he lowered his arms and put the boys back on the ground. Aaron heaved a sigh of relief, then looked around to see where the trophy was. One of the other monkeys still had it in his hand.

"Now we have to get them to play," Aaron said to Aryeh, and then he added, "I know." He ran over to the tree where they'd been sitting. He came back with a small rock which he tossed to Aryeh.

"Catch!" he yelled.

Aryeh caught the rock.

"Throw it back," Aaron called.

Aryeh did.

Aaron caught the rock, ran around, and threw it back to Aryeh. Aryeh caught it, did a few dance steps, and tossed it back.

"Maybe they'll play catch with us," Aaron called, "and throw us the trophy by mistake."

The monkeys squealed and pointed.

They started throwing the trophy back and forth, and running around. One of them even tried to do dance steps like Aryeh.

Aaron started to think. The monkeys were copying them!

Again he threw the rock to Aryeh. Aryeh threw it back. This time Aaron clapped his hands after he threw the rock. The two monkeys playing catch threw the trophy, then clapped their hands.

"They're copying us, Aryeh!" Aaron exclaimed. "I've got an idea!"

Aryeh clapped his hands after he tossed the rock back.

"What?" he asked.

"Just let me get them in the habit of

copying first," Aaron called. He tossed the rock, then stamped his feet. The monkeys tossed the trophy, then stamped their feet. Aaron tossed the rock, then waved his arms. The monkeys copied him perfectly. They were hooting and hollering and having lots of fun. The next time Aryeh threw Aaron the rock, Aaron called out to him, "Watch them closely. If this works, be ready to grab the trophy!"

"Right!" Aryeh called back.

Aaron took the rock, placed it on the ground, then did a handstand. He couldn't see what was happening, but he was holding his breath hoping it would work.

"I've got it, I've got it!" Aryeh screamed. "They've put the trophy down so they could copy you and stand on their hands."

"Run," hollered Aaron, "run and hide

under a bush." Aaron continued to stand on his hands to give Aryeh a chance to get away. Finally, he jumped back onto his feet. Aryeh was gone and so was the trophy. The monkeys were still standing on their hands.

"Pssst," Aryeh called, "over here."

Aaron scampered over to Aryeh, who was hiding in between two thick bushes. Aaron dove in beside him just as he heard the monkeys screech in frustration.

"We did it, we did it!" Aaron exclaimed. "We did it!"

Aryeh was grinning from ear to ear. "I knew you could help me," he declared. "I just knew it!"

The monkeys were screeching and hollering.

"Uh-oh," Aaron grimaced, "looks like it's not over yet! We may have the trophy, but how on earth are we going to get out of here? The monkeys sound like they're really mad."

The screeching and hollering was getting worse and worse as the monkeys realized their precious golden toy was gone. *And* their new talking, dancing dolls were gone too!

But the boys just stayed where they were until slowly the monkeys began to look for them farther and farther away.

As soon as the boys felt it was safe, they ran to find Safari Bill. He was sitting right where they'd left him. They showed him the trophy. He was pleased, of course, although sad they hadn't let him help.

The boys put his leg on and helped him up.

"Well," said Aryeh, "if we hurry I'll get to the race on time."

"I don't think we're going anywhere

quite yet, lads," Safari Bill said softly.

"Why not?" Aryeh asked.

"Look!" answered Safari Bill.

Coming toward them, making a nasty hissing noise, was a huge yellow-and-gray python big enough to eat them all in one gulp.

Aaron was terrified. Was he going to end up as a snake dinner? And his parents would never even know what happened to him. He pulled out his gun. This was his chance. He'd save himself and his friends. He took aim.

Aryeh saw what he was doing.

"No, Aaron, don't!"

Aaron fired!

10
BROKEN!

The gun blast was so powerful that Aaron fell over backwards. When he scrambled to his feet, he gasped. The python lay in a heap of Lego blocks. Safari Bill was bending over it, tears streaming down his face.

"Oh, no," he wailed, "look what you've done to this beautiful creature. You've broken him!"

Aryeh glared at his friend.

"I warned you not to use that," he said.

"But," Aaron protested, "that snake would've eaten us!"

"Nonsense," Safari Bill said. "I've

lived all my life in this jungle, never been eaten yet. We could've outrun it, or I could've thrown my net over it." And he showed Aaron a large net attached to his backpack.

Aaron felt terrible. He looked at the snake, now just a bundle of Lego blocks, and he felt like crying. He'd thought using his gun would make him feel so brave, but he realized he didn't feel brave at all. In fact, it was the opposite. He'd behaved just like a coward — he'd only shot because he was afraid. He walked over to the pile of Legos.

"I'm sorry," he said. "I really am. You were right, Aryeh. It's just — I always thought a safari hunt would be so exciting! I'd seen it in the movies so much and on TV. But it's not like that at all." He looked at his gun. Then, piece by piece he took the gun apart until it, too, lay on the grass in little pieces. "There! I never want to have another gun again!" he declared.

"We could put the snake back together," Safari Bill suggested.

"Really?" Aaron asked.

"But it would take a lot of work and time," Aryeh said, "and I must go. I have to get to the race!"

"Well, you go ahead, young lad," Safari Bill said. "I'll take care of young Aaron here. He and I will repair this snake while you go on to your race."

"I think that is a good plan," Aryeh agreed. "Will you guide Aaron back to the hotel before morning when he gets big again?"

"Yes, I will," Safari Bill agreed.

Aryeh grinned at Aaron. "Don't feel too bad," he said. "You helped me get the trophy — I couldn't have done it without you! I can't tell you how much it means to me that Mother will never know I lost it."

"I'm glad you came to get me," Aaron replied. "It certainly was an exciting adventure — and I learned something, too."

"Now, young Prince," Safari Bill said, "can you see the little path?"

Aryeh looked down and noticed a narrow path where the grass was slightly shorter. He never would have noticed it unless it had been pointed out.

"Oh yes!" he said, surprised.

"I travel the jungle so often," Safari Bill explained, "that I've made many different paths. Just follow this one and you'll soon find yourself at the edge of the Safari Park."

"And I can find my way from there," Aryeh said.

"Well, good-bye," Aryeh called as he hurried off.

"Good-bye," Aaron called. "Hope your wing is better soon!"

Aryeh gave one last wave and disappeared behind some trees. Aaron was sad to see him go. They had become best friends so quickly, and he knew it would be a long time before he could see him again.

"Well," Aaron said to Safari Bill, "let's get to work!"

Fortunately, Aaron was very good at putting Legos together. He and Safari Bill worked quickly, and before long the snake began to look like its old self. They left the head until the last.

"How are we going to put his eyes and mouth in without him attacking us when he's finished?" Aaron asked. Already the body was beginning to slither around, making it hard for them to work on the head. Safari Bill ended up sitting on the body to keep it still while Aaron worked.

"Well, lad, I suggest we leave the mouth for the last. I'll hold it open while you put in the last blocks. Then we run for it!"

Aaron agreed. His heart started to pound. He was frightened, but he knew he couldn't stop. He *had* to put the snake back together. Aryeh was right. The snake had as much right to be there as he did. More, actually. After all, Aaron was just a visitor in the snake's jungle.

This would take all his skill. Quickly he reached to the ground and put the snake together block after block. The mouth was almost finished. The snake started to hiss.

"Get a move on, lad," Safari Bill

yelled. "It's a python. It can crush us as easy as eat us."

"But I have some blocks left!" Aaron cried.

"Go, lad!" Safari Bill screamed. "Now or never!" So Aaron dropped the blocks and Safari Bill leaped off the snake, and they ran! The python slithered and hissed behind them, but when Aaron turned around, it was no longer following them.

"Well, lad," Safari Bill chuckled, "it'll be a snake with a bit of a gap in its lower lip but it's practically as good as new."

He slapped Aaron on the back. "Now let's get you home!"

Aaron opened his eyes. The room was quiet. He looked at his watch. 9:15 A.M. His parents and his sister must have gone to breakfast while he'd slept right through all the morning hustle and bustle! But he wasn't surprised.

He'd been exhausted by the time he got back to his room. He and Safari Bill had run away from gnus, more giraffes, and just as they were leaving the park, the vulture had swooped down on them and almost scared them to death! But he'd gotten back to the palace safely, had grown big, and had slipped back into his bed without anyone noticing he'd been gone.

He sat up and realized he was still in his clothes. He decided to change and go find his family. He was hungry.

As Aaron was changing his pants, he felt something in his pocket. He pulled out a tiny shiny silver bottle with a gold top. On it, a note was attached. He pulled the note off and read the little letters.

Dear Aaron,

I didn't want to wake you again so I'm writing you this note. I came in second in the boat race! And the winner was so happy to see his name added to the trophy. Thanks again! In the bottle is the shrinking potion, so if you come back, you can come and visit me without an invitation — because you are always invited!

Your very good friend,

Aryeh

P.S. Safari Bill refuses to leave my side — he says we saved his life so he will stay with me forever. I'll have to let him save my life back or I'll go crazy!

Aaron carefully placed the little bottle in his knapsack. He hoped it wouldn't be too long before he got to use the potion on his next visit to Legoland.

Aryeh's note had fallen to the ground. Aaron picked it up and read it again. He laughed as he tucked it into the knapsack. Poor Aryeh — followed around by Safari Bill forever!